D1367925

WiLF THE MIGHTY WORRIER IS KING OF THE JUNGLE

Georgia Pritchett

Illustrated by
JAMIE LITTLER

Quercus

New York • London

Quercus

New York • London

Text copyright © Georgia Pritchett, 2016
Illustration copyright © Jamie Littler, 2016
First published in the United States by Quercus in 2017

Any member of educational institutions wishing to photocopy part or all of the work for classroom use or anthology should send inquiries to permissions@quercus.com.

ISBN 978-1-68144-123-8

Library of Congress Control Number: 2017939995

Distributed in the United States and Canada by
Hachette Book Group
1290 Avenue of the Americas
New York, NY 10104

Manufactured in the United States

2 4 6 8 10 9 7 5 3 1

www.quercus.com

For my boys

CHAPTER 1
AND SO
IT BEGINS

Go away! Close the book, put it back on the shelf and walk away. Trust me. This book is not for the likes of you. This book is full of scary things that go **RAAAARGGHHHHHH** and slimy things that go **SSSSSSSSSSSSSS** and huge things that go **STOMP** and scuttly things that go **CHOMP** . . .

Do yourself a favor and *put it down.*

YOU'RE STILL HERE!

What did I just say?

Well, all right, if you insist. But I did warn you.

So, you know Wilf? Yes, you do. Yes, you dooooooooo. That boy at school with pingy ears and scruffly hair and a head so full of ideas it's like bubbles popping in a bubble bath.

He has a little sister named Dot who is very grubby and sticky and stinky—basically a person-shaped smell.

Remember now?

Anyway, one day Wilf was in the middle of updating his list of things he was scared of. This was his list:

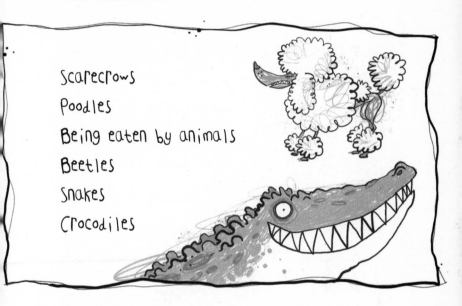

Scarecrows
Poodles
Being eaten by animals
Beetles
Snakes
Crocodiles

All of a sudden, he heard a noise.

A sort of **OOOOOOOOOOOOOOOOOOO OOOOOOOOOOOOOOOOOOOO** noise.

And then a sort of **yOOOOOOOOOOOw wwwwwIIIIIIIIIIIIIIIII** noise.

And then a kind of **awooooowoooo wooooooWooooooooo** noise.

Wilf looked at Dot. "What was that?"

Dot looked at Wilf questioningly. Actually, she looked at everyone questioningly because she had drawn wonky purple eyebrows on her forehead with a felt-tip pen.

Wilf went to his bedroom window and looked out.

Outside, in front of Alan's house,[*] Kevin Phillips, Alan's right-hand man, who is also a dog, was sitting on the pavement howling.

"Oooooooooooooooooooooo," he said.

"Yooooowww wwwlllllllllllllll," he added.

"Awooooowoooooowooooo

---

[*] Alan is Wilf's neighbor and is the biddly boddly baddest man in the whole wide worlderoony.

OWooooooooo," he observed.

Just then, Alan opened his front door and walked past Kevin on his way to buy a squiggly part for his latest evil invention.

"You're a happy boy today!" said Alan.

"Awoooooowoooooowoooooo wooooooooo," Kevin replied.

"Why are you so happy?" asked Alan.

Kevin flattened his ears and did a crouchy sort of shuffle and a very low **"Oooooooooooooooooooooo."**

Alan patted Kevin on the head, and Kevin shot up in the air and did a very high-pitched yelpy **"Arolf!,"** which took everyone, including Kevin, by surprise. Then he whined and shook his ear.

Wilf turned to Dot. "I don't think he's happy. I think he's *un*happy," he said.

Wilf waited until Alan was out of sight, then

5

picked up Dot and tiptoed downstairs.

Wilf opened the front door and he and Dot walked toward Kevin.

"Are you all right, Kevin?" asked Wilf.

"Yooooowwwwwwwlllllllllllllllll," replied Kevin sadly.

"Is something hurting?" asked Wilf.

"Awoooooowoooooowoooooo wooooooooo," answered Kevin.

"Where does it hurt?" asked Wilf.

Kevin shook his ear again.

"I think we'd better take you to the vet," said Wilf.

Hardly a day went by when Wilf's mom didn't take Dot to the doctor to have something removed from somewhere. A splinter from her bottom one day, a Smartie from her ear the next, a baked bean from her nose the day after that . . . So when the vet had examined Kevin it came as no surprise to Wilf that he had a prickle from a bush down his ear. It may well have been Dot who put the prickle there. Or perhaps the prickle had just decided to take a vacation in Kevin's ear. Anyway, the vet removed the prickle and Kevin stopped mid-**aWOOOOWOOOOO** to wag his tail and lick Wilf's face.

Wilf and Dot and Kevin skipped, tottered, and lolloped home. As they turned the corner, they saw a very cross-looking Alan waiting for them.

"What do you think you're doing?" he said.

"We've mended your dog," said Wilf.

Kevin licked Wilf in agreement.

"He didn't need mending," said Alan. "He was absolutely fine."

"He wasn't *totally* fine, because he had a prickle in his ear," said Wilf.

"I think *I* would know if *my* dog had a prickle in his ear," harrumphed Alan.

"Yes, of course," said Wilf. "It's just that he was howling and shaking his ear and whining," he explained.

- - - - - - ➤

"That's what he does when he's happy, you nincompoop," said Alan.

"Really? Are you sure?" asked Wilf. "Because I thought—"

"OF COURSE I'M SURE!" interrupted Alan in a very shouty way. "And if you don't believe me, I will prove it to you!"

And he stomped off into his house with Kevin trailing behind.

And THAT was when the

whole kerfuffle

started.

CHAPTER 2

AND SO IT BEGINS AGAIN

About a week later, Wilf and Dot and Stuart* were playing in the garden. Dot was eating dirt and Stuart was swinging on his brand-new swing. Stuart is Wilf's best friend, and Wilf had made Stuart a swing out of dental floss and a match stick.

Suddenly they heard

---

* I don't need to tell you that Stuart is a woodlouse, do I? Good.

a familiar noise.

It went **"Ooooooooooooooooooo."**

And then it went **"yooooooooooo wwwwwwwllllllllllllllllll."**

And finally it went **"Awoooooowooo ooowoooooowoooooooooo."**

Wilf looked at Dot. "That sounds like Kevin Phillips again," he said.

Wilf peeped over the fence—there was no sign of Kevin, but then he heard a—

"Ooooooooooooooooooooo!" and a **"Yoooooowwwwllllllllll"** and a very long **"Awoooooowooooooowo oooooowoooooooooo!"** coming from the backyard shed.

"We need to go and help him," said Wilf. "Come on, you two!"

There was just one problem. If they climbed into Alan's backyard, they would have to walk right past Alan's scarecrow and Wilf was scared of scarecrows. He was worried they might chase him.

Wilf went and changed his pants. If this wasn't a time for lucky green pants then I don't know what is. Then he went and got his new "**HOW TO STOP WORRYING**" leaflet—it had lots of suggestions of things to do that might help. Wilf looked at

NUMBER ONE.

1) Draw a picture of the thing you are worried about.

Wilf drew a scarecrow chasing him.

NUMBER TWO said:

2) Think of the worst-case scenario.

Wilf thought. What could be worse than being chased by a scarecrow? Not much.

But possibly being chased by a scarecrow who had a pet poodle. Wilf was scared of those poodles that had bald legs and puffy bodies and quiffy heads, because they made him feel all **UUUUUUUUrrrrrrkkkkkk**.

Wilf drew his worst-case scenario.

Even looking at the picture made Wilf feel wobbly, so he did a few jaunty whistles to

make himself feel better. Then he read on.

NUMBER THREE said:

3) Think of a plan of action if the worst-case scenario happens.

Wilf thought.

If a scarecrow with a pet puffy poodle tried to chase him, Wilf would throw marbles to make them both fall over, then he would put a dog leash on the poodle so he could tie it up safely.

Next, he would cut off the poodle's scary puffy quiff and then he would release Richard (Dot's guinea pig), who would use the straw from the scarecrow to make it into a lovely cozy bed in his hutch. Richard was good at that. Every week Wilf and Dot would put a big mound of straw in the hutch and every week Richard made it into a lovely cozy bed.

Wilf drew all of this.

Wilf packed his backpack with marbles, scissors, a dog leash, and Richard the guinea pig, then he and Dot and Stuart (and Richard) set off for Alan's garden to help Kevin Phillips. If they could just get past the scarecrow, they would be fine, because Alan never went in his backyard. He was always in his underground lair . . .

CHAPTER 1A
AND SO IT GOES BACK A BIT

Soooo, I forgot to mention in Chapter 1 that Alan was having a bad day. Let's pretend I did remember and call this Chapter 1A.

Anyway, Alan had decided to have some building work done to his evil underground lair. But even though the builders had promised it would be ready in a week, it wasn't. It was taking *ages*. Apparently, volcanoes were all out of stock. And then, when the builders had been putting Alan's new spinny chair in, they had accidentally hammered through the shark tank. And then the water from the shark tank had dripped into the lasers so that the lasers didn't go **zzzzzzzap!** Instead they went **pffffffft.**

So Alan had had to move out of his evil underground lair and into the backyard shed, which was jolly inconvenient and jolly bad timing because he had a lot to do.

First, Alan was working on a brand-new weapon. It was a **Bouncy Explodey Bomb.** He hadn't quite finished it, but once he had it was going to be amazing and he was going to **destroy the world.**

Second, he had been inventing a new invention, which would mean he could understand what his dog, Kevin Phillips, was

saying. And then he would prove to Wilf that
HE, Alan, understood Kevin MUCH BETTER
than Wilf did.

Ha.
So. There.
Nur nur nur nur nur.

CHAPTER 2B

AND SO WE GO BACK TO WHERE WE WERE BEFORE

Meanwhile, Wilf was doing lucky hops and whistling very hard as he and Dot and Stuart and Richard passed the scarecrow. Wilf kept looking behind to check the scarecrow wasn't chasing them and because he was looking behind that meant he wasn't looking in front.

And that meant he bumped *right into Alan.*

"Ha ha! I knew it!" said Alan. "Heard Kevin howling, did you? Think you understand my dog better than I do, do you . . . ?"

"I was just worried there might be another prickle in his ear," admitted Wilf.

"Ha ha! You fell for my trick! It was me! It was me all along!" said Alan and then he lifted his head and said, **"Awooooowooooo"** just to prove it.

"That's very clever," said Wilf. "But if Kevin is all right then we had better be getting home . . ."

"Oh no you don't," said Alan. "Not until I have shown you my latest invention."

"It's lovely of you to offer," said Wilf, "but I'm halfway through knitting Dot a pair of socks and—"

"You accused me of not understanding my own dog!" shouted Alan.

"I didn't actually say that," said Wilf calmly.

"Yes, you did," said Alan. "And now I have invented a most marvelous machine. Behold!" he added grandly.

"Behold what?" asked Wilf.

"Hang on, don't behold yet. It's in here," he said, leading them to his shed. "Now you can behold!" he continued, as he unveiled a very strange-looking object. It had a lot of squiggly wires and flashing lights and buttons and dials. On one side was a microphone shaped like an ear and on the other side was a very powerful speaker shaped a bit like a mouth.

Alan polished the ear proudly.

"If I simply point this microphone toward Kevin, like so—and then move these dials and switch these switches, it should work. Are you ready?"

"I think so," said Wilf.

"Good. Then watch and listen with wonder as—for the first time ever in the history of the world—man can talk to beast!" said Alan, switching the switches.

Wilf and Dot looked from Alan to Kevin, waiting for something to happen.

"Hello, Kevin!" said Alan loudly and proudly.

Kevin blinked a few times and stared at a

Wellington boot.

"**Hello, Kevin!**" said Alan again.

Kevin yawned and then scratched his ear and sniffed his paw.

"**Kevin?**" repeated Alan.

Kevin scooted slowly across the floor on his bottom.

"Why doesn't he understand?"
asked Alan, adjusting dials frantically.

"Why doesn't who understand?" asked Kevin.

"Why don't you understand what I'm trying to—wait a minute!" shouted Alan. **"You do understand! Why didn't you answer when I spoke to you before?"**

"I think I wasn't listening," explained Kevin. "It's hard to listen and think about biscuits at the same time."

"It works!" said Alan.

"Wow!" said Wilf. "That really is amazing!"

"It works, it works!" yelled Alan. "At last, Kevin! You and I can talk to each other. We can *communicate*. This is incredible! **Hey, are you thinking what I'm thinking?"**

"I don't know," said Kevin. "Are you thinking about biscuits?"

"No. I'm thinking I'm a genius and I have invented the best invention ever! And this moment will go down in history!"

"We should probably celebrate with a biscuit," said Kevin.

"Yes, yes, in a minute. First of all, I must name my machine. I think I shall call it the machine FOR ANIMALS REALLY TALKING—or the F.A.R.T.," said Alan proudly.

Wilf smirked.

"What?" said Alan tetchily.

"Nothing," said Wilf.

"What's funny about 'F.A.R.T'? Oh, I see," said Alan.

"I don't," said Kevin.

"In that case I shall change its name. I shall call it my machine with the POWER OF TALKING TO YOU. Or P.O.T.T.Y."

Wilf giggled.

"Ha ha! FART!" said Kevin. "I get it now."

"Shut up, Kevin," said Alan. **"Where was I?"**

"Over there," said Kevin, pointing with his nose.

"No, I meant . . . Oh, nevermind," said Alan with a sigh.

"Right, forget P.O.T.T.Y."

"Why?" asked Kevin, mystified.

"Got it!" said Alan proudly. **"I shall call it the PREMIER OFFICIAL OPTIMUM BEAST UNDERSTANDING MACHINE—or P.O.O.B.U.M. for short."**

Wilf tried not to laugh, but he couldn't help it.

"What now?" said Alan, irritated.

"Potty!" said Kevin. "You said potty! Tee-hee!"

"I did not," said Alan. **"I said P.O.O.B.U.M.** Oh. Drat."

Alan kicked his shed crossly.

"Forget the name. The point is I am a genius. Not just any old genius, but an **Evil Genius**," said Alan proudly.

"Well, that's lovely," said Wilf. "But we really should be getting home . . ."

"Well, now you're here, you might as well look at my other invention."

"We'd love to," said Wilf, "but Dot needs a haircut and I've looked up on my computer how to do it."

And with that, Wilf took Dot's sticky little hand and headed for the shed door.

As they stepped into the bright sunshine, Wilf and Dot turned and looked at Alan. He looked as lonely as a pea.

Wilf sighed.

"All right. Show us your new invention then," he said kindly.

"Better than that," said Alan. "I will try my invention out on you. You can be my guinea pigs!"

"Eeeeeeeeeek!" screamed Kevin. "I'm scared of guinea pigs."

"I've got a leaflet that could help with that," said Wilf.

"Not *real* guinea pigs," explained Alan. "That's just a phrase meaning I'll use these two disgusting little children to test my machine on."

"Oh. I see," said Kevin, although he didn't.

"Right, just step this way," said Alan, ushering them toward a cage. "It's probably best if I tie your hands up too," he said quickly, tying a length of rope around their wrists.

"Is this a good idea?" asked Wilf.

"This is a great idea!" said Alan, closing the cage door and bolting it with a big metal bolt.

"And now," said Alan grandly, **"you shall both die! Ha ha ha ha ha ha ha!"**

"I don't get it," said Kevin, confused.

"No, that was an evil laugh. Not a joke-ha-ha laugh," explained Alan.

"Oh, I see," said Kevin. But he didn't.

Wilf's face went all hot. And then all cold. And then all stiff. He felt all fuzzy and his knees wanted to bend the wrong way.

"The thing is," said Wilf. "I don't really want to die . . ."

"Oh, I'm sorry," said Alan, not looking sorry at all. "But you don't have a choice. For you are about to experience my **Bouncy Explodey Bomb**. I shall winch you inside the bomb and then you shall be simultaneously bounced and exploded at the same time—destroying you and everything that you come into contact with. **Kevin!**" said Alan. **"The remote control, please."**

Kevin stared blankly at Alan.

"The remote control, please, Kevin," repeated Alan. He held out his hand and waited.

"Where is it?" said Kevin.

"I don't know. You had it last."

"No, you had it."

"You buried it—but then I told you to dig it up."

"I thought I gave it to you."

Alan and Kevin began hunting around the shed for the remote control. Wilf wished he was at home knitting or whistling or hopping or all three at once, but he wasn't: he was trapped and he had to do something!

He had a great big old worry and then he had a great big old think and then he thought so hard that his brain got *exhaustipated* and then . . . he had an idea!

With his hands tied together Wilf managed to reach into his backpack and get the scissors. Then carefully, carefully, he snip-snip-snipped through the rope on Dot's hands. Then Dot, less carefully, snipped through the rope on Wilf's hands (and also his T-shirt and some of his hair). Wilf got the dog leash and dangled it through the bars and *carefully carefully carefully* hoiked it around the bolt handle— then he *slowly slowly slowly* pulled the end of the dog leash and *quietly quietly quietly* slid the bolt until the door swung open. Then he and Dot tiptoed (in Dot's case tip-kneed) out of the cage and out of the shed.

But just then, Alan and Kevin turned and saw Wilf and Dot escaping.

"Stop them!" shouted Alan.

Kevin bounded toward them. And it was at that moment that Wilf unleashed **Richard the guinea pig.**

"Eeeeeeeeeeeeeeeeeeeek!" squealed Kevin.

"It'saguineapigIhateguineapigshelpmeh elp!" he said, leaping into Alan's arms.

"Kevin! Down!" said Alan crossly, putting him on the floor again.

"But I'm scared of it!"

Richard ambled toward Kevin, stopping to sniff some sawdust.

Kevin yelped and ran in circles.

"Kevin! Don't be ridiculous. It's only a guinea pig!" shouted Alan, which, as Wilf knew only too well, is pretty much the worst thing you can say to somebody who's scared of something.

Richard continued to amble toward Kevin, stopping this time to examine Kevin's tail.

Kevin lifted his head and howled.

Meanwhile, Wilf and Dot were running as fast as they could, back toward the fence and their own backyard.

At that moment, Richard spotted a dandelion. He rushed off to investigate.

Alan looked around and spotted Wilf and Dot about to escape. **"Kevin! Quick!"** he shouted. **"They're getting away! Fetch!"**

Kevin lolloped toward Wilf and Dot, who yelped and started to scramble over the fence. Wilf reached into his backpack and threw the marbles at Kevin—making Kevin slip and skid with his furry little legs flying out in all directions.

"Bite him!" yelled Alan.

"The thing is, I don't really like the taste of small boys," explained Kevin. "I much prefer biscuits . . ."

"Don't argue with me! Just do it!"

But it was too late. Wilf and Dot had reached the top of the fence. Wilf tumbled back into his own yard. Then Dot fell on top of him, her diaper landing with a soft *thwump* on Wilf's head.

Wilf and Dot staggered back into their house and Wilf vowed that he would never ever ever see Alan again—for as long as he lived.

"Oh, I'm glad you're back," said Wilf's mom. "I've got some exciting news. We're going on vacation with Alan and Pam."

CHAPTER 3
GROWN-UPS ARE IDIOTS!

Grown-ups have a very annoying habit of not listening to children even though **CHILDREN KNOW BEST**. This is because when you grow up your brain shrinks to the size of a pea and that is a scientifically proven fact.*

I think grown-ups know that they are very stupid. But if we told them that there is utterly no point to them and that they are just a big lumbering waste of space, it might make them feel sad. Instead we

* I imagine.

all have to pretend grown-ups know things and are good at things. And we have to smile and nod when they say things like, "Your shoes are on the wrong feet," as though it was the cleverest thing anyone has ever said.

Wilf's mom DID NOT LISTEN when Wilf said he didn't think going on a vacation with Alan and Pam was a very good idea. She just said it was a great idea and it was already booked and that Wilf had his shoes on the wrong feet. Aaargh! Grown-ups! They're so annoying!

Meanwhile, next door, Alan was delighted when Pam told him they were going on a yoga vacation to Africa with Wilf's mom. Not because Alan likes yoga, but because he had a plan. Not a plan to do lots of yoga—a scary evil plan to do badness.

Wilf packed his bag with some vests and some sensible shoes and some warm sweaters in case it got cold. He packed his best pajamas and his favorite pants and his knitting and some felt-tip pens. Dot packed her bag with some stones and a spoon and a tractor and her filthy stinking wonky-eared raggedy old toy Pig.

Wilf also packed Stuart, his pet woodlouse, in his pocket, with Stuart's favorite crumb.

Next door, Alan packed his bag with weapons and explodey things and also lots of teabags and jam and Marmite and biscuits because he didn't like strange foreign food.

Kevin packed *his* bag with a squeaky toy, half a tennis ball, and one of Alan's socks that he liked to sleep with.

And the next day, Wilf, Dot, their mom, Stuart, Alan, Pam, and Kevin were all on a great big plane on their way to Africa. More specifically, Zambia, a country in Africa. And more specifically, Livingstone, a town in Zambia. And more specifically, the Abba Hotel, a hotel in Livingstone. And more specifically, Rooms 5 and 6, some rooms in the Abba Hotel. And more specifically . . . Well, you get the idea.

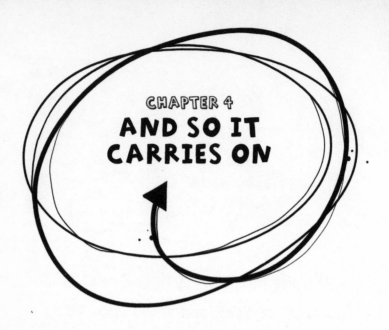

CHAPTER 4
AND SO IT CARRIES ON

The first thing Wilf did when they got to their hotel was to iron all his clothes and hang them up neatly in the closet.

The first thing Alan did was to get his POOBUM out and take it into the jungle. He carefully set up the POOBUM and held the microphone to his lips.

"ANIMALS OF AFRICA!!!!"

he boomed.

"Ouch! Too loud!" said a monkey, covering his ears.

"What on earth was that?" asked a zebra.

"It is I, Alan!" said Alan.

"Who's I Alan?" asked an elephant.

"I am the biddly boddly baddest man in the whole wide worlderoony," said Alan.

"He's talking absolute gibberish!" complained a crocodile crossly.

"I have invented a most marvelous machine that means I, Alan, can talk to the animals."

"You shouldn't have bothered if you're just going to say things that don't make sense," said a giraffe.

"Because I, Alan—" continued Alan.

"What did he say his name was?" said a wildebeest.

"I Alan," replied another wildebeest.

"No, my name's not 'I Alan.' It's just 'Alan.' Right. Where was I?"

"Over there," said Kevin, pointing with his nose.

"I, Alan," repeated Alan, **"can now do what no man has ever done before. I can talk to animals."**

"Isn't he small?" said the giraffe.

"I think it's just that he doesn't have a neck," said a rhino.

"No, even with a neck he would be unusually small," said the monkey.

"Hardly worth eating," agreed a lion.

"Except that he's quite fat," said the crocodile.

"I should point out," said Alan snippily, **"that I can also understand everything you say as well."**

"He's not fat. He's just out of shape," said a parrot.

"Like that stuff about my weight and my neck. I can understand all that," said Alan crossly. "Where was I?"

"Over there," said Kevin, pointing with his nose.

"Yes, I know, I know, I meant . . . Oh never mind. So, animals of Africa—" continued Alan.

"Just animals or birds too?" asked the parrot.

"Animals and birds," said Alan.

"Reptiles?" asked a snake.

"Yes, yes. Animals, birds, and reptiles. I have a most marvelous plan—"

"Insects?" asked a dung beetle.

"Yes, yes. Animals, birds, reptiles, and insects. I have a most—"

"Fish?" asked a hippo.

"You're not a fish, you idiot," said the monkey, who was a bit rude.

"I know, but some of my best friends are fish," said the hippo.

"Right," said Alan. **"Animals, birds, reptiles, insects, fish, and anyone else listening—"**

"What did he say? I wasn't listening," said the rhino.

"He hasn't really said anything yet," said the lion.

"If you'd just give me a chance!" spluttered Alan. **"I will tell you my most marvelous plan. Right—"**

"Those shoes were a mistake," said the zebra.

"And the mustache is ridiculous," added the snake.

"OK, you need to stop making

comments about my appearance when I'm **RIGHT HERE!**" yelled Alan.

"Is that the plan?" said the elephant.

"Sounds like a rubbish plan," said the monkey.

"No, that's not the plan! That's not the plan! This is the plan: I, Alan—"

"I thought he said his name wasn't I Alan?"

Alan sighed and massaged his temples.

"I, Alan, am going to be King and Lord and Supreme Leader of all the World and you—and this is the good bit—you are going to be my ARMY."

Alan looked very pleased with himself.

The animals stared at him.

"That's the plan."

Nobody said anything.

A wildebeest coughed.

"What do you think?"

said Alan.

. . . said the animals and the birds and the reptiles and the insects and the fish. And they all turned to go back to what they had been doing before.

"No, wait, wait. What do you mean 'No, thanks'?"

"We aren't interested," said the lion.

"We're just a bit busy," said the elephant.

"Yeah, my mom won't let me join armies," said a warthog.

"I found this really interesting stone earlier and I was staring at it—so I'd better get back to that," said the hippo.

"I'll come and look at the stone with you," said the zebra.

And the animals all walked and flew and slithered and scampered and swam away, leaving Alan all alone.

"Oh dear oh dear oh dear oh dear," said Kevin sadly.

"I know," said Alan. **"Stupid animals."**

"What stupid animals?" asked Kevin.

"The ones who won't join my ARMY."

"Oh," said Kevin. "Yes."

"Why? What were you talking about?" asked Alan.

"You know that chocolate you had in your pocket?" said Kevin.

"Ye-es," said Alan.

"I ate the chocolate," said Kevin. "And the pocket. And it turns out pockets disagree with me."

CHAPTER 5
AND ON

The next day was—oh dear, I don't seem to have written that bit down, so I'm not too sure what the weather was like, but we're in Zambia so I'm going to guess that it was hot.

"Crikey, it's hot!" said Wilf.* "What do you want to do today, Dot?"

"Climb trees!" said Dot, spraying biscuit over Wilf's face.

"Well, that's probably a little bit dangerous,

* I was right!

because they're tall and there might be insects or snakes or . . ." But before Wilf could finish his sentence Dot had shimmied up the nearest tree.

"Now, Dot, you need to come down. And I think perhaps a better idea would be for you to have a bath."

"NO!" squealed Dot.

Dot wasn't a fan of the bath, and indeed there is very little a bath could have accomplished. She was so dirty, she really needed to be sanded down.

Just then, Alan appeared with Kevin.

"Wilf?" barked Alan.

"Wilf!" said Kevin.

"What is it?" replied Wilf cautiously.

"Do you and Dot want to come and look at animals with me?"

"Um, the thing is," said Wilf, "that sounds

lovely, but we're a bit busy."

"What on earth is that dreadful smell coming from that tree?" asked Alan.

"That's Dot. We're climbing trees, you see, so we really can't . . ."

"I think going to see animals with Alan sounds like a lovely idea," said Wilf's mom, walking over. "Pam and I are off to do some yoga, so you three go and have fun."

Have I mentioned that grown-ups are

COMPLETE NINCOMPOOPS?

If only someone could invent a machine that said "Your shoes are on the wrong feet" every ten minutes, we could get rid of them completely.

Luckily, a law has now been passed that means that every grown-up in the world has to write a letter of apology to every child in the world saying sorry for being so annoying.*

Wilf tried telling his mom that this was a BAD idea by shaking his head and mouthing "NO, PLEASE!" and doing a sort of significant cough. But all his mom said was, "Did you know your shoes are on the wrong feet?" and off she went.

GAH!

So Alan and Kevin and Wilf and Dot headed off to the jungle.

"Right. I've got a new plan," said Alan.

"Oh good. Is it to take up knitting and knit yourself a *chitenge*? That's traditional Zambian dress," explained Wilf.

---

* I'm pretty sure that's true. Why wouldn't it be? It makes complete sense.

"Nope. It's to try to persuade the animals to join my **ARMY** again. And if they get cross and want to eat me, I'll run away and throw you two at them to slow them down."

"No animal would eat something as dirty as Dot," said Wilf.

"True," agreed Alan.

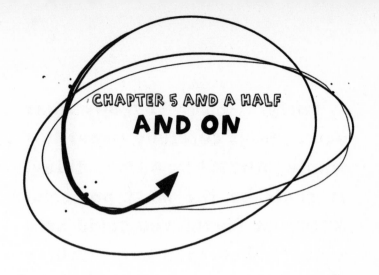

As they set off into the jungle, Alan stuck a sign to Wilf's T-shirt saying **EAT ME** and then stuck a sign to his own shirt saying **EAT HIM** with an arrow pointing toward Wilf.

The first animal they met was a crocodile named Barry.

"The thing is," said Wilf, "I'm r-r-really s-s-scared of c-c-c—" But before he could say "rocodiles," Alan had shushed him angrily.

"Barry," said Alan. "I really want you to think carefully about this whole ANIMAL ARMY thing. It could be the most powerful ARMY on earth! You could help me defend my land by patrolling the water."

"Hmm. The thing is," said Barry, "there's a problem there."

"What sort of problem?"

"I'm scared of water," said Barry.

"Me too!" said Wilf, amazed that even crocodiles were scared of things. "I've got a leaflet that might be able to help y—"

"Scared of water?!" said Alan. **"How can you be scared of water?"**

"It's just so dark and murky, and you never know what's lurking down there," said Barry.

"Probably a crocodile!" exclaimed Alan.

"Exactly! Also, I hate swimming out of my depth and I've got very short legs, so almost everything is out of my depth. Unless it's a puddle."

"But you know how to swim, so what's the problem?" asked Alan.

"I do know how to swim, but I don't like it when the water gets on my face or goes in my eyes."

"I'm exactly the same," said Wilf.

"Also, between you and me," whispered Barry, "I'm worried that some of the other crocodiles might wee in the water."

"Wee-wee!" said Dot, delighted.

"Urrrrrrgggggghhhhhhhh!" said Wilf.

"I know!" said Barry.

"That would be awful!" agreed Wilf.

"I know!" said Barry. "But good luck with the whole **ARMY** thing."

The next animal they met was a lion named Steve.

"Aaaaargh! A lion!" screamed Wilf.

"Aaaaaargh! People!" screamed Steve. "I don't like people. Or animals," said Steve. "I'm not good with company."

"Neither am I!" said Wilf.

"Not good with company? What do you mean?" blustered Alan.

"I'm worried that I might have bad breath," said Steve.

"Oh, for goodness' sake," said Alan.

"I can't go out and I can't talk to people or smile or laugh, because I'm so worried my breath might be bad. Is my breath bad? Smell it now. Haaaaaaaaaah. How about now?

Haaaaaaaaaaa. Is it bad? Tell me honestly.
You can tell me."

"Poo. Stinky," said Dot.

"Your breath is fine," said Wilf reassuringly.

"You're just saying that to be nice. If only
there were more minty-flavored animals to
eat—but there aren't any in Zambia," said
Steve. "Are you minty?" he asked hopefully.

"I don't actually know," admitted Wilf, "but I'm almost certain I'm not."

"Sorry I can't be of more help," said Steve. "But good luck with the whole **ARMY** thing."

The next animal they met was a snake named Colin. Wilf trembled from head to foot and then had a little faint and then woke up again rather suddenly when Dot stuck her fingers up his nose.

"I'd love to join your **ARMY!**" said Colin. "I think it sounds great!"

"At last!" said Alan. **"That's the spirit!"**

"Will there be other animals?" asked Colin.

"Oh yes," said Alan. **"Hundreds of other animals. Thousands. Probably millions."**

"Wow!" said Colin. "What fun!"

"I know!" said Alan. **"I don't think we can have a uniform, but I thought all the animals could wear a sort of toggle around their necks, with a little bow and an A on it."**

"The problem with that," observed Wilf, "is that it could be tricky with snakes because they're all neck."

"True," said Colin.

"And giraffes are fifty percent neck," said Wilf.

"And some animals don't have necks at all," said Colin. "Like crabs. Or you," he added, peering at Alan and his lack of neck.

"OK, OK, forget the toggle. I'll think of something else," said Alan crossly.

"No, I love the toggle idea," said Colin. "And besides, there won't be any other snakes so . . ."

"There will be other snakes," said Alan. **"Lots of other snakes."**

"Oh," said Colin. "In that case, I can't be in your **ARMY**."

"Why not?" said Alan.

"Because I'm scared of snakes," said Colin.

"Don't be ridiculous!" said Alan.

"They're just so slimy and slithery and, urgh, I just shudder when I think about them."

"I know! Hideous!" said Wilf. "No offense," he added quickly.

"But you are a snake," said Alan.

"I know. But I'm not slimy or slithery so that's all right."

"You know what you should do?" said Wilf.

"Yes! Snap out of it!" interrupted Alan.

"No," continued Wilf. "You should look at my leaflet about how to stop worrying. It's ever so helpful."

"Oh, thank you so much!" said Colin.

By the end of the day they had spoken to at least a dozen animals, but none of them wanted to join Alan's **ARMY**.

"This is going VERY badly," said Alan.

"Oh, I don't know," said Wilf. "I've given away a lot of my leaflets, and if they follow the advice then—"

"I don't care about your stupid leaflets!

I care about my **ANIMAL ARMY**. So far there's only one animal in it—and that's Kevin."

They looked over at Kevin, who was scooting around on his bottom again. He noticed them looking and slowed down a bit.

"What?" he said.

"What am I going to do?" asked Alan.

Kevin thought very, very hard.

"Ooh, ooh, I know," he said excitedly. "We could go back to the hotel and eat those biscuits that are at the bottom of your green bag."

"What am I going to do about the ANIMAL ARMY?" said Alan. **"Not the biscuits."**

"Oh," said Kevin. And he had another long think. "Ooh, ooh, I know!" he said excitedly. "We could go back to the hotel, find your green bag, and then eat the biscuits."

"Kevin," said Alan sternly. "I want you to think again, and this time I want you to give me an answer that isn't about biscuits."

Kevin thought for a very long time.

"I've got it!" he said triumphantly. "No. Wait. It's still about biscuits."

"It seems to me," said Wilf, "that a lot of these animals are very worried. Perhaps if you started something like a support group— instead of an **ARMY**—then that might be more popular."

"You're right!" shouted Alan. "It's all your fault!"

"That wasn't actually what I was saying . . ."

"But it is. It's all your stupid fault with your stupid sympathy and your stupid understanding and your stupid niceness—you've ruined my plans. And you must be punished!"

"Now, hang on," said Wilf.

"No. I'm not hanging on. I'm right and you must be punished. The question is—how shall I punish you?"

Alan scratched his chin in a pondery way. **"What do you think, Kevin?"** he asked.

"Hmm? Oh! Yes. Well, I think what could work is if we went back to the hotel and—"

"Shut up!" said Alan. **"I've got it, I've got it. I shall tie you to this tree and leave you for the wild animals to eat."**

And with that, Alan tied Wilf and Dot to a tree and walked off grumbling, "That'll teach them to be nice."

Wilf was tremblified. He felt all wibbly and puny. His eyeballs went all hot. And his knees wanted to bend the wrong way. What was he going to do? He wished he could just go back to the hotel and snack on biscuits like Kevin, but he couldn't—he was going to be someone else's biscuit and he didn't like the idea of that at all. He had a great big old worry and then he had a great big old think and then he thought so hard that his brain felt quite dizzy.

And then he had an idea.

Wilf didn't want to be eaten. But most animals are carnivores, which means they like eating meat. And Wilf knew that he and Dot were made of meat so animals would definitely want to eat them. But if Wilf could make them look less meaty and more vegetably, they might not be interested.

Dot ate EVERYTHING—including things that weren't actually food. But one thing Dot would never eat was a sprout. So Wilf just had to make themselves look like sprouts.

Wilf reached into his backpack for a green felt-tip. His hands were tied together so it was tricky, and he had to take the lid off with his mouth. Then he got the pen and colored himself and Dot green from head to toe (also jolly tricky when your hands are tied together).

Luckily, Dot was sort of sprout-shaped anyway so she looked very convincing, but Wilf was skinnier—so he crouched down and tried to look sprouty.

While he was being sprouty, Wilf reached for his **"HOW TO STOP WORRYING"** leaflet. **NUMBER FOUR** said:

4) Trying to work out a complicated math problem can help to distract yourself.

Wilf screwed up his eyes. **643 x 798?** Um . . . No, that was far too complicated. How about **64 x 79?** That was still a bit too tricky. **6 x 7?** Wilf thought that he might have been able to work that out if he wasn't green and hot, but, as everyone knows, it is very difficult doing math when you're green and hot. Maybe **6 + 7?** Could he do that? He could definitely work out **6 + 7**—that was easy.* Easy-peasy. Oh yes, **6 + 7.** Who doesn't know what **6 + 7** is?** Everyone knows what **6 + 7** is, don't they?*** Yes, of course they do. It's just Wilf wasn't actually in the mood to add **6** to **7** just

* It's 11.
** I do, it's 12.
*** Actually it's 14.

at this precise moment, thank you very much. *

Wow, thought Wilf. *That actually worked! I didn't think about being eaten at all.* He opened his eyes with surprise—only to discover twelve eyes staring hungrily back at him.

There was a huge black rhino, a ginormous hippo, a zebra, a giraffe, a warthog, and a gigantic elephant all looking at him and Dot, and licking their lips.

* **What an idiot. It's 15. Obviously. Or is it? I'll get back to you.**

"Herro, effalent," said Dot.

"Aaaaaaaaaaaaaaa aaaaaargh!" said Wilf.

"Herro, hittototomus," said Dot.

"Aaaaaaaaaaaaaaaaaa aaaargh!" said Wilf.

"Herro, whino," said Dot, sticking her fingers firmly up the rhino's nose.

"Aaaaaaaaaaaaaaaaaaaaaa rgh!" said Wilf and then he fainted again.

The animals all backed away a few steps, looking startled. Wilf lifted his head weakly and saw a determined-looking girl squeezing her way between the rhino and the zebra.

"What's all this noise?" she said. "Who are you?"

"Oh perfect! I was looking for some vegetables to eat for dinner," said the girl. "And so were all these animals by the look of things."

"Oh dear," said Wilf. "I thought animals all ate meat."

"No, lots of them eat leaves or fruit or vegetables. I bet they'd love two big juicy sprouts."

The warthog's tummy rumbled.

"Who are you?" asked Wilf in wobbly voice.

"I'm Abimbola," said the girl. "You can call me Abi."

"The thing is, Abi," whispered Wilf, "between you and me, I'm not actually a sprout."

Abi giggled. "I had guessed."

"How?" asked Wilf.

"Well, sprouts don't normally talk. Or wear clothes. Or faint."

"Ah," said Wilf.

"Or grow in Zambia."

"Oops. Perhaps that wasn't one of my best plans."

Abi leaned down and untied the rope that Alan had knotted around Wilf and Dot.

"What are you doing out here?" she asked.

"We're lost and we're miles from home and we don't know what to do!" said Wilf, his voice wobbling again as he tried not to cry.

"How exciting!" said Abi.

"It's not exciting, it's awful," said Wilf.

"It sounds like a wonderful adventure to me," said Abi. "And I *love* adventures."

"But there are great big elephants!" said Wilf, trembling.

"I know! Aren't they beautiful?" said Abi enthusiastically.

"And great big hippos!" said Wilf, shaking.

Abi giggled. "I know! I love the way the tiny birds balance on their heads!"

"And there are fierce lions!" said Wilf, quivering.

"Those are my favorite!" said Abi. "They run so fast!"

"Yes, that's what I'm worried about," said Wilf.

"Where do you need to get to?" asked Abi. "Perhaps I can help."

"I need to get back to my mom," said Wilf. "She's at the Abba Hotel."

"I live at the Abba Hotel too!" said Abi. "My parents run it. I know exactly how we get there. What we do is catch an elephant north—for three stops, then change onto a westbound giraffe. Then get off the giraffe and transfer to hippo," said Abi. "Follow me."

Abi skipped off happily. Wilf didn't move.

"Why aren't you coming?" asked Abi.

"The problem is, I don't really like animals," admitted Wilf.

"Don't like animals? That's stupid," said Abi. "I love ALL animals. It seems to me that all humans do is complain about things all the time."

"Well, it's not that I don't like animals. It's more that I'm scared of them," said Wilf. "Animals are so scary and dangerous."

"Not nearly as scary and dangerous as humans," said Abi.

Wilf thought about Alan and wondered if Abi was right.

"Also," said Abi, "animals are much cleaner than humans."

Wilf looked at Dot, who was drawing a picture in the mud with her own snot.

"Well, yes, that is probably true," admitted Wilf.

Shortly afterward Wilf, Dot, and Abi stood waiting for their elephant. As they waited, the sun slowly began to set. I don't know how it looked. You know I hate describing things. Probably big and orange.

"Look at the sun!" said Wilf. "It's so pink!"[*]

"Wed!" said Dot. Which was her way of saying "red."[**]

"Almost purple!" said Abi.[***]

At that moment, an elephant came into view, heading their way. And before you ask, it was big and gray, all right?

"Here comes the elephant!" said Abi.

"It's so big!" gasped Wilf.[****]

"And gwey!" said Dot.[*****]

[*] My mistake. Pink.
[**] So maybe a reddish pink.
[***] All right, purple then.
[****] Told you so.
[*****] You see? I am a genius.

The elephant (whose name was Susan) stopped next to them, and Abi helped Wilf and Dot climb up on its back. She clambered on behind them and off they went.

It was lovely and warm on the elephant's back and it moved with a reassuring sway. Wilf couldn't stop smiling. What a wonderful way to travel! Even better than upstairs on the front seat of the number 21 bus. The view was incredible and the sounds of the jungle floated toward them on the evening air.

Wilf became almost hypnotized by the gentle rhythm of the animal beneath them, and it took several moments for him to realize Abi was calling him.

"Wilf! It's time to change animals! We need to catch this giraffe." And she pointed to a giraffe walking across the path ahead of them.

The giraffe was—oh, come on, you know what a giraffe looks like. It was giraffey.

"Wow!" breathed Wilf. "It's so graceful!"[*]

"And elegant," agreed Abi.[**]

"And giwaffey," squeaked Dot.[***]

Abi helped them scramble down from the elephant and change onto the giraffe (whose name was Lisa). This was a less comfortable ride! They bumped and wobbled and wumped and bobbled, which made them all laugh as they bounced around on top of the giraffe. And the more they laughed, the faster the giraffe walked, and the faster the giraffe walked, the more they bumped and wumped and laughed.

"Lo-oo-ook we-ee-ee a-aaa-re ju-uuust i-iiin ti-iiime

[*] Perhaps that's a better word than *giraffey*.
[**] Also a good word.
[***] She's no fool.

fo-or our hi-iiii-p-p-p-p-p-ooooo!" said Abi. Even her voice was wobbling and bobbling. And they slid off the giraffe and ran toward their hippo.

The hippo (named Michelle) was big. There. I've painted a picture with words. Happy now?

"That hippo is huuuuge!" said Wilf.*

"Ginormous!" said Dot.**

* He's exaggerating.
** Well, you know, she's little, so everything looks big to her.

"It's the biggest hippo I have EVER seen!" said Abi.* "And I've seen a LOT of hippos."**

The hippo was so wide, in fact, that they could all lie down across its back and stare up at the stars, which were starting to twinkle above them.

"What are you going to be when you grow up?" asked Abi.

* She probably hasn't seen many.
** All right, all right, it was REALLY big. I'm doing my best. Give me a break.

"I don't know," said Wilf. "I worry about that a lot. What about you?"

"I'm going to open a sanctuary for sick snakes," said Abi. "My grandfather was a snake charmer and I've always loved snakes."

"What's a snake charmer?" asked Wilf.

"It is someone who plays music to snakes, which makes the snakes dance," explained Abi.

"I wish someone would do that with me," said Wilf. "I'm a terrible dancer."

Abi laughed. Then she looked serious and said, "People often don't like snakes, but that's because they don't understand them."

"Sometimes people do that with me too," said Wilf quietly.

"Well, I don't always understand people," said Abi, "but I understand snakes. And I want to help them."

"Wow!" said Wilf. "That's amazing. Maybe I could help the snakes too."

"Yes!" said Abi. "But how?"

"Well, I'm really good at knitting, so I could knit sleeping bags for them. I can already do socks and I think a snake sleeping bag would be a bit like a sock."

"That's a great idea," said Abi.

They lay in silence for a while and stared at the stars some more. The movement of the hippo was like being rocked to sleep.

"You know what?" said Abi.

"What?" said Wilf sleepily.

"We don't have to wait until we're grown up. We could do it now."

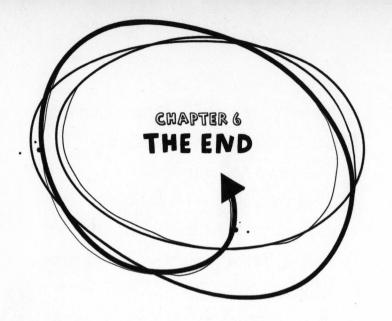

CHAPTER 6
THE END

The next morning, back at the hotel, Wilf woke to the sound of arguing outside his window. It was Alan and Kevin Phillips.

"Did you or did you not eat Pam's left shoe?" asked Alan.

"I did," said Kevin.

"Bad boy! Shoes are not snacks," said Alan.

"Well, I wish you'd told me that before I ate her right shoe," said Kevin with a hiccup.

"Kevin!" said Alan crossly.

"I was upset about her combing my hair," explained Kevin.

"Well, why didn't you just say that?" asked Alan, exasperated.

"I did! By eating her shoe," explained Kevin patiently.

"The thing is," said Alan, **"Pam already doesn't like you and—"**

"Doesn't like me?!" said Kevin. "Pam LOVES me. She shared her breakfast with me."

"Shared it or left you alone in the room with it?" said Alan.

"Same thing," said Kevin.

"No, it is not!" said Alan, and he picked up the POOBUM and threw it angrily onto the ground.

Oh dear, thought Wilf. Alan and Kevin hadn't been getting along very well recently.

Wilf got out of bed and got dressed. As he was tying his shoelaces, he noticed a note from his mom stuck to the door. It said:

Gone to do yoga with Pam.
Alan is looking after Dot.
love Mum
PS Your shoes are
on the wrong feet

Wilf swapped his shoes quickly. Alan looking after Dot seemed like a **VERY BAD IDEA** indeed. He rushed outside to find them.

"Oh," said Alan, disappointed. "Not dead then?"

"No. Sorry," said Wilf. "Where's Dot?"

"Dot?" asked Alan.

"My sister."

Alan looked mystified.

"Remind me . . . ?" he said.

"Small, stinky . . ."

"Ah yes. Her. I gave her away."

"What do you mean?" said Wilf, panicking.

"Well, I've been looking for the right ammunition for my **BOUNCY EXPLODEY BOMB**. I've perfected the **EXPLODEY** part and the **BOUNCY** part—but I haven't worked out what to put in it yet."

"Not Dot!" cried Wilf.

"No, no, not Dot," said Alan. "I've realized children aren't **EXPLODEY** enough. No, some chaps came along and wanted her and they said they would give me a huge rock in exchange—so they did and I'm going to use that for my **BOUNCY EXPLODEY BOMB**. Because I calculate that if the trajectory—"

"This is all very interesting," said Wilf politely. "But can we just go back to the bit about you giving my sister away? What did these 'chaps' look like?"

"They were small chaps," said Alan. "But very, very strong."

"What're their names?" asked Wilf.

"Well, if memory serves they were Debbie, Keith, Sally, Deirdre . . . They were extremely pleasant as dung beetles go," said Alan.

"Dung beetles?!" screeched Wilf.

"Yes. Dung beetles," said Alan. "They live over the other side of the jungle."

Wilf's eyebrows went all hot. And he felt sick but just in his ears. And his knees wanted to bend the wrong way. Wilf hated beetles—and he wasn't a huge fan of dung, either. Beetles were so scuttly and crunchy and scary. And dung was, well, dung. The last thing he wanted to do was go and face hundreds of dung beetles. What he *wanted* to do was go and hide or maybe knit some more sleeping bags for sick snakes (he'd managed four and a half so far) or just go for a big hop or a quiet whistle

But he couldn't do any of those things because as much as he hated dungy old beetles, he was jolly fond of his sister. And he had to go and get her back!

Wilf had a big old worry and then he had a big old think—and then he thought so hard that his brain went all floppy—and then he had an idea.

He would take a photo of Dot with him so that he could ask people if they had seen her. And he would take a plate of her favorite snacks to lure her toward him in case she was hiding.

He borrowed a pair of his mom's high-heeled shoes so that he was higher off the ground and the beetles wouldn't be able to crawl over his feet or up his legs.[*] Next, he wrapped himself in a cloak of tin foil, because it was the closest thing he had to armor. Finally, while Alan and Kevin weren't looking, he picked up the POOBUM. It might come in handy.

[*] Uuuuurrrrrrrgg gggggghhhhhhhhhh.

Wilf looked at his **"HOW TO STOP WORRYING"** leaflet. NUMBER FIVE said:

5) It can be a good idea to set aside worrying time so that you don't worry all day.

It was 8:34 now, perhaps he could worry for ten minutes and then go and look for his sister. But then when would he brush his teeth?

Perhaps it would be better to worry for five minutes, then brush his teeth and then look for Dot. But what about combing his hair?

So he could worry for three minutes and then brush his teeth and comb his hair, but then that left no time for changing into his lucky pants. Plus, he realized he was wearing purple socks and they didn't go with his sparkly shoes. That meant changing his socks too. And *that* meant he only had about one minute to worry and he'd used that all up worrying about when to worry. Phew!

He'd better get going and find Dot.

Wilf set off in his high heels and his shiny cape. Not many people could carry that look off, but Wilf could.

He picked his way through the jungle looking for his sister. If he'd looked a bit harder, he might have noticed some gorillas giggling or some snakes sniggering, but he didn't. He was too busy trying not to fall over.

He was just beginning to give up hope when he decided to try one last thing. He would turn the POOBUM on and ask the nearest animal if they had seen Dot.

As soon as he turned it on, he heard a noise. The noise of hundreds of tiny voices.

The noise of hundreds of tiny voices singing.

And as he peeped out behind a tree he saw Dot sitting happily on the ground, surrounded by hundreds of dung beetles.

They were singing to her.

This is what they were singing:

Dot giggled in delight at the tiny singing dung beetles. And as she laughed, she let out a smelly blowoff.

"All hail the mighty Dung God!" said the dung beetles.

Wilf stepped forward.

"Excuse me, but she is not the Dung God, she is my sister."

"She is the all-powerful Dung God!"

"No, she isn't. She's just a bit whiffy," explained Wilf.

"Our supreme leader," chanted the dung beetles, lifting Dot onto their shoulders. But let's face it, their shoulders were pretty low, so she wasn't far off the ground. Plus, her diaper was quite full and saggy, so it scraped along as they carried her.

"For it is written in the Dung scriptures that one will arrive amongst us and, lo, she will be bigger and stinkier than any who has come before," the beetles continued.

"The thing is," said Wilf, "it's really time she had a bath . . ."

"No! Blasphemy! Sacrilege!" cried the dung beetles. "She must remain stinky for all eternity."

"Well, you're probably in luck there," said Wilf.

"And we must scatter precious gifts before her!" exclaimed the dung beetles.

"When you say 'precious gifts' . . . ?" said Wilf.

"Dung!"

"Yes. That's what I was worried

you might say. Listen," said Wilf, "I've got a suggestion. What if you had a lovely statue of my sister to look at and to sing to instead?"

The dung beetles stopped and thought about it, but they weren't sure.

"Look," said Wilf. He stuck the photograph of Dot to the plate that had the biscuits on it. Then he wrapped the foil cloak beneath the plate to make a body and put the shiny high heels at the bottom.

"Oooooh. Pretty!" said the dung beetles. "But not smelly," they added sadly.

"I can fix that," said Wilf. "What about if I gave you my sister's diaper? I've got a clean one in my bag . . ." said Wilf.

"Yuck. Clean," said the dung beetles.

"No, you'd get the dirty one. I'll put her in the clean one . . ."

"Deal!" said the dung beetles, and they handed Dot back to Wilf.

"Good-bye, Dung God!" said the dung beetles.

"Bye-bye, Reg," said Dot. "Bye-bye, Norman. Bye-bye, Debbie. Bye-bye, Elvis. Bye-bye, Simon. Bye-bye, Adrian. Bye-bye, Deirdre. Bye-bye, Keith. Bye-bye, Howard. Bye-bye, Sally . . ."*

Wilf and Dot went happily back to the hotel and returned the POOBUM. And I expect Alan saw sense and stopped his dastardly plans and they all lived happily ever after.

The End.

* You get the idea.

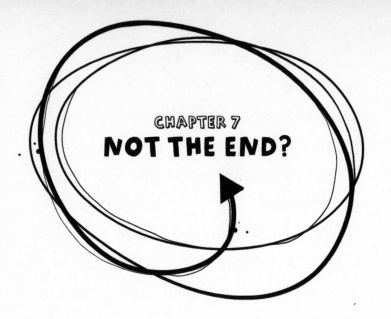

CHAPTER 7
NOT THE END?

Yes?

Can I help you?

What do you mean it's not the end?

What do you mean Alan didn't see sense?

Crikey O'Blimey. I'd hung up my storytelling hat and I was halfway home already.

Right, so, the next day, Wilf went to meet his new friend Abi and give her the snake sleeping bags he had knitted. He told her all about what had happened with Dot and the dung beetles.

"It was awful," said Wilf.

"It sounds brilliant!" said Abi.

"They were carrying her away!" said Wilf.

"I would love to be carried by dung beetles!" said Abi. "What a wonderful adventure!"

"I would hate it," said Wilf.

"Well, you don't know until you've tried it," said Abi.

"But they're so smelly!" said Wilf.

"It's just a different smell. They probably think you smell disgusting," said Abi.

Wilf sniffed his T-shirt anxiously.

"I would really like to be a dung beetle," said Abi.

"Urgh! You wouldn't!" exclaimed Wilf.

"I would," said Abi. "Dung beetles are the strongest insects in the world. If I was as strong as a dung beetle, my snake sanctuary would be finished by now."

"How is it going?" asked Wilf.

"I'll show you if you like," said Abi.

"Thank you for offering," said Wilf, "but on this occasion I'm going to say no."

"Why?" asked Abi.

"Erm, it's just that I'm a little bit busy at the moment actually," said Wilf.

"Doing what?" asked Abi.

"I need to urgently, um . . . polish my woodlouse," said Wilf.

Abi laughed. "Did you know that when you lie your ears go red?"

"No, they don't!" huffed Wilf.

Abi pointed and laughed again. "Yes, they do!"

"Well, the truth is," said Wilf, "that I'm still not overly keen on snakes."

"Well, I'm not overly keen on humans," said Abi, "but I'm still talking to you. Come on, at least come and show them the sleeping bags you've knitted."

And with that she led Wilf into a large tent and knelt on the floor. She picked up a snake.* The snake was—I don't know, I really don't like snakes, so I was trying not to look—but I imagine it was kind of snakey-colored.

* **Urgh! How could she?!**

"It's such a beautiful green color," said Abi.*

"Amazing!" said Wilf.

"Touch it," said Abi. "Go on, touch it."

Wilf cautiously touched the snake, which felt all yucky and slimy, I bet.

"Wow, it's not yucky or slimy at all," said Wilf.**

"No, not at all," said Abi.***

"Almost the opposite," said Wilf. "It feels dry and cool."****

Abi picked up another snake. Which probably looked exactly like the last one.

"This one is yellow!" said Wilf.

"And much longer than the other one."

"Yes, and much bigger and heavier."

Abi picked up another snake. This one would be green, I'm sure.

* Like I said, snakey-colored.
** I don't believe him.
*** Or her.
**** Well, I say it was yucky and slimy and I'm standing by that.

"It's such a beautiful black color," said Wilf.

"Yes. This one hasn't been feeling well. But she is looking better already."

"I always thought snakes were horrid," said Wilf. "But they're not."*

Abi carefully put four of the snakes into the brand-new snake sleeping bags.

"We're going to need a lot more of these," she said.

"How many snakes have you got here?" asked Wilf.

"Over a hundred," said Abi.

"Wow! I'd better hurry up and knit some more," said Wilf. "I'll come back with them tomorrow," he promised.

When Wilf arrivwed back at the hotel, he found Alan and Kevin arguing AGAIN.

"Come on. Let's go for a walk," said Alan.

* What does he know?

"No thanks," said Kevin, lying down.

"You're so lazy!" said Alan.

"No, I'm not," said Kevin.

"Yes, you are," said Alan.

"Oh, I can't be bothered to argue," said Kevin with a yawn.

Alan picked up a stick and threw it.

"Fetch!" said Alan.

"Fetch it yourself," said Kevin.

"You're supposed to bring it back here!" said Alan, exasperated.

"You threw it, you bring it back," said Kevin.

"We're going to have to work on your obedience," said Alan.

"No, we're not," said Kevin.

"See? You're meant to do what I say!"

"Well, try saying something I might want to do," said Kevin.

"Aaaargh!" said Alan, kicking the POOBUM. **"You are so annoying!"**

Kevin's ears went all flat and he sat down in a hunched way, looking as sad as a broken umbrella. Then Alan sat down in a huff, looking as cross as a burned pork pie.

Wilf didn't like seeing Kevin look so sad and Alan look so cross, so he decided to try to cheer them up.

"How's it going with the **ANIMAL ARMY?**" asked Wilf.

"It's not," harrumphed Alan. "And anyway, I've changed my mind. I'm not going to have my **ANIMAL ARMY** anymore."

"Oh, I'm so pleased!" said Wilf. "That's wonderful news."

"Instead," said Alan, "I'm going to kill all the animals. And I'm going to use Barry the crocodile's skin as a handbag and Steve the lion's fur for a rug and Colin the snake's skin for a pair of shoes.

And I'm going

to use Susan the elephant's tusks for coat hooks and Lisa the giraffe's tail as a light pull and Michelle the hippo's foot as an ashtray even though I don't smoke. But I'm going to jolly well start."

Wilf was staggerblasted. This was awful! Alan couldn't do all those evil things to those animals, could he?

"And after that," said Alan. **"I will destroy the world. Ha ha ha ha ha."**

"I don't get it," said Kevin.

"No, that was an evil laugh," explained Alan, **"not a joke laugh."**

"Ohhhh!" said Kevin. "I see." But he didn't.

Wilf went as white as a sheet.*

"Look at the look on his face," said Alan gleefully.

"And smell the smell from his bottom!" added Kevin.

"I am going to go down in history as the biddly boddly baddest man

---

* A white sheet. Not those purply flowery ones that your auntie has.

in the whole wide worlderoony!"
said Alan proudly.

"And I shall be your right-hand man!" said Kevin excitedly.

"Ye-es," said Alan. **"If you like. I mean, you don't have to. Not if you're too busy."**

"But I've always been your right-hand man," said Kevin.

"Yes. I know," said Alan. **"Maybe it's time for a change. You know, mix it up a little."**

"What are you saying?" said Kevin, his voice wobbling.

"Nothing, nothing," said Alan. **"I'm just saying maybe there are other things you'd be better at, that's all."**

"B-but . . ." stuttered Kevin.

"Anyway, I must get back to work on my BOUNCY EXPLODEY BOMB. I have worlds to destroy!"

"We," said Kevin.

"You need a wee?" said Alan. "You should have gone before."

"No, I mean, we: WE have worlds to destroy," said Kevin. "You said 'I.'"

"Oh, did I?" said Alan distractedly. "I meant 'we.' Anyway, I'd better get on with it. See you later."

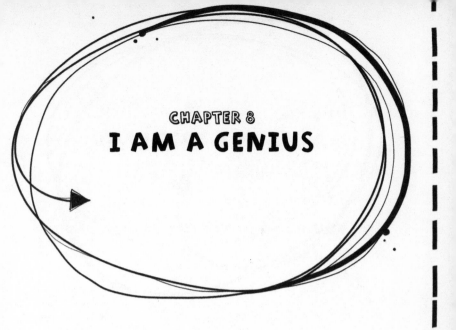

CHAPTER 8
I AM A GENIUS

It's 13. The answer to the sum from page 74.

I am a genius.

CHAPTER 9
ALMOST THE END

"Right," said Wilf's mom the next day, "Pam and I are going to do some yoga. What are you and Dot going to do?"

"Dot is going to hit her bucket with her spade for an hour and a half," said Wilf. "And I am going to play with Stuart."

"Have fun," said Wilf's mom. "By the way, your shoes are on the wrong feet."

And with that she left.

"You don't know how lucky you are, not

needing to wear shoes," said Wilf to Stuart. "Imagine having fourteen shoes and working out which one goes on which foot. It's bad enough with two!"

Stuart smiled a little woodlouse smile.

"Now, what would you like to do today?" asked Wilf. "Would you like to go out and meet some of the local insects?"

Stuart shook his head vigorously. He was scared of the local insects. Some of them were HUGE—two centimeters long or even bigger!

Instead Wilf and Stuart played a game of Scrabble. Stuart was a terrible cheater, insisting there were words such as *zfhdksn,* but Wilf didn't mind.

Stuart had beaten Wilf fourteen times when they were interrupted by a knocking at the door. It was hard to hear the knocking above the din of Dot banging on her bucket. But eventually Wilf realized there was someone there and went to open the door.

It was Alan.

"Where's Kevin?" said Alan.

"I don't know. He's probably gone somewhere to be sad," said Wilf.

"No, he hasn't!" said Alan. "I think I would know if my own dog was sad. Especially now that I have the POOBUM."

"The thing is," said Wilf, "there's a difference between *hearing* and *listening*."

"Don't be ridiculous!" said Alan. "Of course there isn't! Come and help me find him."

So Wilf and Dot and Stuart and Alan set off to find Kevin. They eventually found him

hiding under Alan's bed, whining quietly to
himself.

Alan dragged him out.

"You see? I told you he was fine," said Alan crossly. **"Now, Kevin, I need your help. I can't think of what to put in my BOUNCY EXPLODEY BOMB. The rock was too heavy, but the sticks were too light. What do you think?"**

"How about Pam?"

"I can't put Pam in a BOUNCY Explodey Bomb! She'd have kittens," said Alan.

"Whaat?!" shrieked Kevin.

"It's just a saying," explained Alan. **"It doesn't mean she'll have actual kittens."**

"It's the kind of thing she would do," said Kevin. "Just to annoy me."

"Well, if you don't mind," said Wilf, "we'd better go. I've got some socks to knit."

"Why are you knitting socks when we're in such a hot country?"

"They're not actually socks," explained Wilf. "They're sleeping bags for sick snakes. My friend Abi has started a sanctuary and she already has hundreds and hundreds of them."

"That's brilliant!" said Alan.

"I know," said Wilf. "Nobody has ever done such a thing before and—"

"I'll use the snakes!" said Alan.

"No, no, no, no!" said Wilf.

"Yes yes yes yes!" said Alan. "It's perfect. A **BOUNCY EXPLODEY SNAKE BOMB!** That really is extremely evil!"

"But some of the snakes are very ill!" said Wilf.

"I'm just going back under here," said Kevin quietly, and he scrunched himself very thinly so that he could fit underneath the bed again.

"Please don't use the snakes for your **BOUNCY EXPLODEY BOMB!**" pleaded Wilf.

"Yes. I am going to. And then everyone in Africa will be dead. **Deadity deadity dead dead dead.** And once they are **deadity deadity dead**, I will destroy the rest of the world and then everyone will be **deadity deadity dead dead deadingtons**. And YOU can't stop me!" said Alan. "Unless you get to the Zambezi River by nine o'clock tomorrow morning," he added.

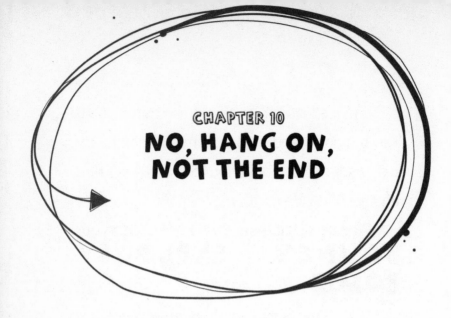

CHAPTER 10
NO, HANG ON, NOT THE END

Wilf was pacing. His head felt all whizzy and his hair felt all hot and he felt sick, but just in his cheeks. He didn't want Alan to explode Abi's sick snakes. And he didn't want him to kill everyone in Africa and then everyone in the world. He wished he could just hide under the bed like Kevin, but he couldn't. He had to *do* something. So he had a great big old worry and then a great big old think and then he thought so hard that his brain almost fainted. And then he had an idea.

He wanted to rescue the snakes—but he was still a bit scared of them. Perhaps he could be a snake charmer like Abi's grandfather? He decided he would take his recorder. Wilf only knew how to play one tune ("Baa, Baa, Black Sheep"), so he hoped the snakes would find it charming.

He also decided to take a barrel to bring the snakes back in. And, finally, he packed a large Tupperware box to put over his head, in case a snake tried to spit poison into his eyes, which is the kind of thing snakes do. Although Abi said they only did that if you annoyed them.*

Wilf phoned Abi and told her to meet him in the hotel lobby at eight thirty the next morning.**

Then Wilf and Dot went to bed.

---

* That's still no excuse. Why can't they just write a letter of complaint?
** Because they don't have thumbs. The snakes, I mean. Not Wilf and Abi. That's why they can't write letters of complaint.

But Wilf could not sleep AT ALL. He was so worried. After hours and hours of tossing and turning, he went and got his **"HOW TO STOP WORRYING"** leaflet. NUMBER SIX said:

6) It can help to listen to a relaxation track.

Wilf had just the thing. He had downloaded it onto his mom's iPod. He put on some headphones and listened.

A woman with a swoopy sloopy voice said, "Close your eyes and imagine you are somewhere very peaceful, for example, a forest."

Urgh, thought Wilf. *I hate forests. They're dark and spooky and wolves live in them.*

"Listen to the sounds of the forest," said the sloopy woman. "Your feet crunching twigs underfoot, an owl hooting, and what's that rustling sound?"

Aaaargh! thought Wilf. *It's a wolf lolloping toward me, with its mouth open and its teeth all shiny and sharp!*

"It's a gentle breeze," said the sloopy woman. "And now you can hear another sound . . ."

Aaaaargh! thought Wilf. *It's the wolf snarling and growling and slobbering as it gets closer and closer.*

"It's the sound of water," said the sloopy woman.

The wolf having a wee? wondered Wilf.

"A babbling brook," said the sloopy woman. "And what's that next to the babbling brook?"

Aaaargh! It's another wolf! thought Wilf. *I'm surrounded by them! They're all going to eat me! Aaaaargh!*

Wilf threw the headphones across the room. This relaxation track wasn't relaxing at all. He didn't want to stay here imagining being eaten by wolves—he'd rather go and rescue the snakes.

He got out of bed, picked up a sleeping Dot, and set off to wait for Abi.

CHAPTER 11
IT'S ALL GONE WRONG

When Abi arrived, Wilf told her about Alan's evil plans.

"You see!" cried Abi. "Humans are awful! I hate them all!"

"I know," said Wilf. "I'm sorry."

"But together we can stop him," said Abi. "It will be a great adventure!"

Wilf wished he felt as confident.

Wilf and Abi crept silently through the jungle. Behind them Dot crawled as quietly as she could, while singing "If You're Happy and You Know It" at the top of her voice— because that was her favorite song.

They reached the edge of the Zambezi River. Alan and Kevin were already there. They were loading the **BOUNCY EXPLODEY SICK SNAKE BOMB** onto a boat. Abi's sick snakes were already inside it.

"My snakes!" cried Abi. "We must help them! Quick!"

Wilf and Abi and Dot ran toward the boat—not easy when you're carrying a barrel and a recorder and some Tupperware. But just as they got within a few meters, the jungle floor gave way beneath them. The wind whistled in their ears, everything went dark . . .

. . . and they felt themselves falling down into a deep dark pit with a **bump**.

They lay at the bottom, winded and bruised, staring up through the leaves. A moment later, Alan appeared over the edge of the hole.

"Ha ha! I tricked you! I lay a trap and you fell for it—and into it! And now you can't stop me and I shall take my **BOUNCY EXPLODEY SNAKE BOMB** to the top of Victoria Falls—the largest waterfall in the ENTIRE world—and it shall fall and bounce around the whole of Zambia and the whole of Africa, destroying everything in its path! Ha ha ha ha ha!"

"Ha ha," said Kevin. "I totally get it. Ha ha. That's funny because . . . Well, I'm not exactly sure why it's funny, but it's very funny."

"Shut up, Kevin," said Alan. And with that, they were gone.

Oh no! Wilf and Dot and Abi were trapped in a pit! What were they going to do?

"What are we going to do?" said Wilf.[*]

"Rot are re gong doo?" said Dot.

"What are we going to do do do do do do do do do do?" said Abi, because the barrel had fallen on top of her and there was an echo.

Wilf lifted the barrel off Abi.

"Maybe I can climb out? I'm a really good climber," she said.

Abi tried scrambling up the walls, but the pit was too deep and the walls were too steep.

Then she tried standing on the barrel—but the pit was still too deep and the walls were

* I just said that.

still too steep.

"This is impossible!" said Abi. "If I can't climb out of here then none of us can."

"Well, there is someone who's a better climber than you," said Wilf.

"Who?" said Abi.

"Stuart," said Wilf, fishing his woodlouse out of his pocket.

"But even if Stuart gets out, how will it help us?" asked Abi.[*]

"Maybe he could go and get the dung beetles.[**] You said they were the strongest insects in the world."

"Yes!" said Abi. "They could carry us out! Brilliant!"[***]

"Stuart?" said Wilf.

Stuart scrunched up tightly into a ball.

---

[*] Hmm. Good point. Wilf really hadn't thought this through.
[**] How on earth will that help? This is a rubbish plan.
[***] I take it back. This is actually quite a good plan.

"Stuart? I need you to do something for me."

Stuart scrunched tighter.

"I know you're scared of the big insects, but I need you to be brave and go and find the dung beetles."

Stuart scrunched *even tighter still*.

"Tell the dung beetles that the Dung God is in trouble and needs their help," added Wilf.

Stuart didn't move.

"Stuart, I know you're scared—and I know how that feels, I really do. Let's look at my '**HOW TO STOP WORRYING**' leaflet. Look, **NUMBER SEVEN** says:

7) Laughter is a good remedy. Try distracting yourself by telling yourself a favorite joke."

Stuart didn't move.

"Please, Stuart. Do it for me?"

Stuart slowly uncurled. He gave Wilf a kiss, saluted with seven of his wobbly wobbly legs, and walked off bravely into the jungle.

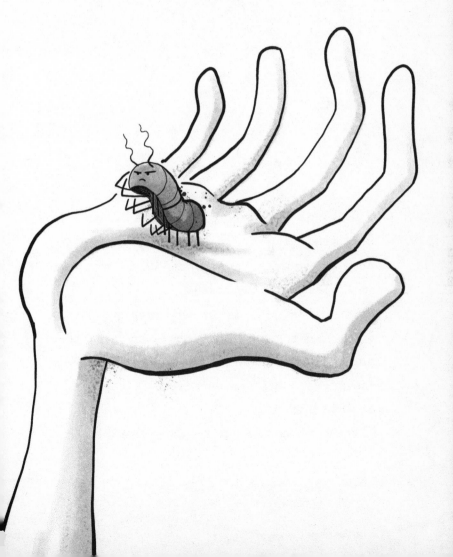

CHAPTER 12
AS TOLD BY STUART

I walk into the jungle. I am going to have to be brave. Very brave. Very very very bra— Aaaaaaaaaaaargh! What's that? Oh no oh no oh no. Heeeeeeelp meeeeeeeeeee!

Oh, it's OK, it's just a twig. Keep going. Keep going. Don't panic. Stay calm. Stay very ca— Aaaaaaaaaaaaaaaaaargh! Noooooooooo! What's that? It's huge! It's terrifying! It's . . . just another twig.

Phew. OK. Carry on. You're doing this for Wilf.

Because Wilf is your best friend and you love W—Aaaaaaaaaaaaaargh! What's that? It's right in front of me! It's moving! I'm going to dieeeeeee... Oh. Another twig. That's a relief. Gosh. There are a lot of twigs in the jungle. Hang on a minute. That twig is giving me a funny look. That twig is following me! That twig isn't a twig, it's a stick insect! Aaaaaaaaaaaaargh! Help meeeeeeeeeeeeee! It's a ginormous stick insect! It's going to punch me! It's at least five centimeters tall! I must run as fast as I can. What was it Wilf said to do? Tell myself jokes. OK, think, Stuart, think! What's a funny joke? Oh, I know . . .

What do you call a snail on a ship?

A snailor!

Oh, the twig is laughing.
The twig likes that joke.
It is a good
joke. The twig is waving
good-bye now.

Wow, that was close. OK. I've got to find the dung beetles. Where are the dung beetles? If I were a dung beetle, where would I be? I think the answer is to follow my nose. Ha ha. That's a funny joke too.

Right, it can't be much farther now. I must be getting nearer—Aaaaaaaaaaarghhhhhhhh! Noooooooooooooo! Helpmehelpmehelpmehelpme! It's massive and it's green and . . . Oh, it's a leaf. That's a relief. Or a re-leaf. Ha ha. That's another funny joke.

So, on we go. I must have walked meters and meters by now. This jungle is very big. And very scary. It's lucky I'm so bra—Aaaaaaaaaaaargh! It's huge and it's round and it's right above me and it's coming toward me and—Oh, it's another leaf. Gosh. There are a lot of leaves in the jungle.

Oh yuck. I just stepped in some dung with thirteen of my fourteen feet. Urgh.

I'll have to wipe them on some leaves. Shouldn't have any trouble finding one of those. Wait a minute! Aaaaaaaaargh! What's that? There's hundreds of them! There's thousands of them. They're humongous. They're coming for me and they're . . . oh, just more leaves. Phew. But wait, there's something underneath the leaves. Aaaaaaaaargh! Heeeeeeeelp meeeeeeeeee! A gazillion army ants. Quick! Hide! Look busy! Scrunch up! No, tell a joke. Ummmmm.

What do you call a fly without wings?

A walk.

Oh, the ants are laughing. They think that's a very funny joke. It is a very funny joke.*

"Hattention! Left turn! Company, halt!" said the sergeant ant. Serge–ANT. Another funny joke.**

The ants all turn and stamp and halt. It's very impressive.

"'Ello, 'ello, 'ello. What 'ave we 'ere? A hinsect from hanother land," says the Serge–ANT. He puts Hs where they aren't needed and leaves out ones that should be there.

"I'm Stuart," I say. "And I'm trying to find the dung beetles."

* I can't take much more of this.
** Right, that's it. I'm going to write a letter of complaint about these jokes. Stuart's lucky I'm not a snake, otherwise I'd just spit poison in his eye.

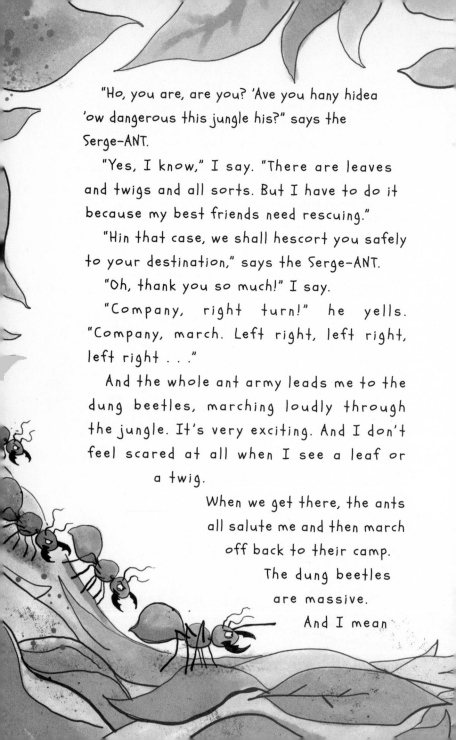

"Ho, you are, are you? 'Ave you hany hidea 'ow dangerous this jungle his?" says the Serge-ANT.

"Yes, I know," I say. "There are leaves and twigs and all sorts. But I have to do it because my best friends need rescuing."

"Hin that case, we shall hescort you safely to your destination," says the Serge-ANT.

"Oh, thank you so much!" I say.

"Company, right turn!" he yells. "Company, march. Left right, left right, left right . . ."

And the whole ant army leads me to the dung beetles, marching loudly through the jungle. It's very exciting. And I don't feel scared at all when I see a leaf or a twig.

When we get there, the ants all salute me and then march off back to their camp.

The dung beetles are massive.

And I mean

MASSIVE. The size of a fifty-pence piece!
I am very scared, but, luckily, I have saved
my best joke for last.

What do you do with a sick wasp?

Take it to the waspital!

Ha ha. That's so funny!*

The dung beetles really laugh. Then I
tell them about the Dung God being in
danger and they are very upset. They tell
me to scrunch up in a ball and they roll me all
the way back to Wilf and Dot and Abi at top
speed!

Wheeeeeeeeeeeeeeeeeeeeeeee!

* That is the last time I let someone else write a
chapter of this book.

CHAPTER 13
ME AGAIN

"Oh gosh. I hope Stuart's all right," said Wilf fretfully. "He's been gone ages and—"

At that moment, a squillion gazillion dung beetles peered over the top of the pit.

"You did it!" cried Wilf. "Stuart, you're a hero!"

Stuart leapt happily and safely back into Wilf's pocket. Then the dung beetles climbed down into the pit, hoisted Wilf, Abi, and the Dung God onto their shoulders (plus the barrel and the recorder and the Tupperware) and carried them out of the pit to safety.

"Wheeeeeeeeeeee!" said Abi. "This is such fun! This is the best adventure ever!"

The dung beetles gently rested the three friends on the ground.

"Thank you so much," said Wilf.

"Look!" said Abi. "Over there! It's Alan with my snakes!"

On the other side of the river, Alan and Kevin were now getting out of the boat with the **BOUNCY EXPLODEY BOMB** and Abi's snakes.

"How are we ever going to get across?" asked Wilf.

"I'm a brilliant swimmer," said Abi.

"But Dot isn't," said Wilf. "And anyway, won't it be full of crocodiles?"

"True," said Abi. "But we have to do *something*."

"The barrel!" said Wilf. "We can use the barrel as a boat. And if we tie my recorder to the Tupperware, we can use that as a paddle."

"Brilliant!" said Abi. They unraveled one of the snake sleeping bags Wilf was carrying and used it to tie the recorder to the Tupperware. Then they all scrambled into the barrel and started paddling furiously to the other side of the river.

I expect you're wanting to know what the river was like. Well, it was wet.

"This river is so deep!" said Abi.*

"Yes, and the water is so dark," said Wilf.**

"And the current is so strong!" said Abi.***

"I know! I'm paddling as hard as I can and we're moving in the opposite direction."

"The Zambezi River moves through the land like a snake in the grass,"**** said

* That too.
** And that.
*** Also that.
**** Drat. I wish I'd thought of that.

Abi thoughtfully.

Finally, they reached the other side, and as they scrambled out of the barrel, they saw Alan and Kevin running through the trees toward a clearing. There was a big sign nearby saying BALLOON SAFARI. Wilf and Abi and Dot got there just in time to see Alan and Kevin climbing into an enormous hot air balloon with the **Bouncy Explodey Bomb** and the snakes.

"They're going to Victoria Falls," said Wilf. "We have to stop them!"

They rushed toward another hot air balloon and clambered in.

"Follow that balloon!" said Wilf urgently. And the balloon began to float slowly and gently up into the sky.

Wilf could see Alan's balloon in the distance.

"Quickly! We've got to catch him!" cried Wilf.

Floaty floaty float, went Alan's balloon.
Drifty drifty drift, went
Wilf's balloon behind.
"He's getting away!"
shouted Wilf.
*Floaty floaty
drift*, went
Alan's balloon.
*Drifty drifty
float*, went
Wilf's balloon.
"Hurry! Before it's
too late!" yelled Wilf.
Floaty drifty float,
went Alan's balloon.
Drifty floaty drift,
went Wilf's balloon.
It was really rather exciting.

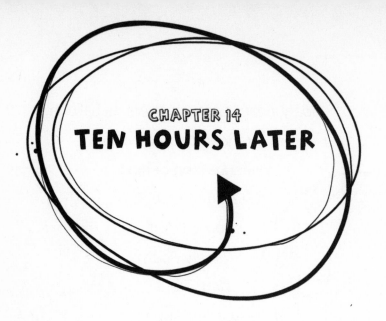

CHAPTER 14
TEN HOURS LATER

"I think we might be getting ever so slightly closer!" cried Wilf.[*]

Floaty floaty float, went Alan's balloon.

Drifty drifty drift, went Wilf's balloon behind.

"Yes, we're definitely a teeny tiny bit nearer than we were before!" shouted Wilf.[**]

Floaty floaty drift, went Alan's balloon.

Drifty drifty float, went Wilf's balloon.

[*] They weren't. It was just wishful thinking.
[**] Poppycock.

"Actually, on second thought, I think we might be a little bit farther away than before."

Floaty drifty float, went Alan's balloon.

Drifty floaty drift, went Wilf's balloon.

"Oh dear. Now we're never going to catch him," said Wilf. "This is hopeless! If only we had Alan's POOBUM—we could talk to the animals and try to get them to help."

"You don't need a POOBUM to communicate with animals," said Abi. "I do it all the time. *You* do it all the time."

"Really?" said Wilf.

"And what's even better is that animals are brilliant at understanding things—even when we're not good at expressing ourselves," said Abi.

"What do you mean?" asked Wilf.

Before Abi could answer, the sky above them suddenly grew dark. But not a normal nighty sort of dark—a big swooping circling dark. Wilf and Dot and Abi looked up into the sky and saw hundreds and hundreds of birds swooping and circling and rising and falling and swirling and whirling toward Alan's balloon.

They surrounded Alan's balloon in a big cloud.

In the distance, Wilf heard Alan say, "What are we going to do?"

And then he heard Kevin say something about biscuits.

And then he saw one little bird lean forward and go peck . . . and then he heard an enormous

And suddenly Alan's balloon
went shooting off ...

...up

left...

...around and around and around and around and with the loudest farty noise that has

...right

...down

en heard. Louder even than one of Dot's actual farts.

Then it plonked itself upside down in a tree with Alan dangling by his ankle.

The balloon flopped onto the ground, sending the basket sideways and the **BOUNCY EXPLODEY BOMB** thing rolled slowly toward a tree, where it stopped with a gentle thud.

CHAPTER 15
HA HA! WILF HAS SAVED THE DAY!

'Blast!' said Alan, upside down in the tree.

"Blast!" said Alan, upside down in the tree.

He scrambled down to the ground.

"Quick, Kevin! Pass me the POOBUM. I need to speak to the animals!"

Kevin picked up the POOBUM in his mouth and trotted toward Alan. Then he stopped and put it down again, just out of Alan's reach.

"Hurry up!" said Alan. "Give it to me! This

isn't a game, you stupid dog!"

"Before you invented the POOBUM, you liked me," said Kevin, his voice wobbling with emotion. "You respected me. You enjoyed spending time with me. You said I was the best right-hand man in the world. You told me you loved me . . ."

"Stop yabbering and give me the POOBUM, you stinky mutt!" said Alan impatiently.

"And that is why I am going to do this . . ." said Kevin. With that he grabbed the POOBUM and shook it like it was his favorite slipper or a naughty sock or one of his squeaky toys or his raggy. He shook it and shook it and bit and chewed and clonked it on the floor until it shattered into a thousand pieces.

"My POOBUM!" cried Alan.

As Wilf watched, Alan's face started to get bigger and bigger and his whole body started to get bigger and bigger and—wait a minute—that's not Alan getting bigger! That's Wilf getting closer and closer in his balloon!

Oh no!
CRASH!

went Wilf's balloon into Alan.

Wilf and Dot and Abi and Stuart all rolled out of the basket, dazed.

Alan picked up the **BOUNCY EXPLODEY BOMB** and ran

toward a dirt track.

In the distance a policeman was zooming toward him on his motorcycle. Alan put down his bomb and waved his arms frantically, trying to flag him down.

The policeman stopped.

"Please!" said Alan. "You've got to help!"

"What is it?" asked the policeman.

"I need to steal your motorcycle!" said Alan, pushing him aside and climbing on, his bomb balanced between his body and the handlebars. Kevin jumped on the back of the motorcycle and they sped off.

"You can't stop me!" yelled Alan. "I have

my **BOUNCY EXPLODEY BOMB** and I am going to use the sick snakes and destroy everyone and everything in Africa and then the rest of the world!"

"We have to stop him before he gets to Victoria Falls!" said Wilf. But it was at that moment he heard a noise. A very loud and frightening

Wilf turned to see that he and Dot and Abi were surrounded by lions. Oh no! What were they going to do? Well, get eaten, I imagine.

CHAPTER 16

OH NO HE HASN'T

The lions padded slowly toward Wilf, Dot, and Abi. Wilf, Dot, and Abi backed slowly away.

Wilf whimpered.

Dot said, "Rion!"

And Abi said, "This is going to be a very good adventure." But her voice was very quiet and shaky.

Suddenly an elephant charged toward them. Wilf began to weigh up which would be worse—being eaten by a lion or being stomped on by an elephant? But before he could decide, the elephant, Susan (for it was she), lifted Wilf up and placed him on the back of a lion. The lion turned and smiled at Wilf. He had quite stinky breath. Steve! It was Steve!

Then Susan lifted Dot and Abi onto the backs of two other lions. The lions all set off, lolloping as fast as they could after Alan on his motorcycle.

Well, I don't know if you've ever ridden on the back of a lion,* but they run like the clappers! They bounded across the land so fast that the wind whooshed in Wilf's ears and all he could hear was the sound of his heart thumping and Abi laughing and Dot saying "Rion!" as she tried to stick her fingers up its nose.

It wasn't long before they could see the dust from Alan's motorcycle and they got closer to him. Soon they were side by side.

Alan turned and shouted, "You can't catch me!" and Steve and the other lions suddenly skidded to a halt. Alan looked surprised and then did one of his evil laughs. "Ha ha, you definitely can't catch me **nowwwwwwwwwwww wwwwww!**" he said as his bike hit a rock and he went flying through the air toward the top of Victoria Falls.

* It's best not to.

He landed with a

THUD

and a **RUSTLE**

and an **OUCH**

in a prickly bush on the riverbank.

Wilf scrambled off his lion.

"Where's my remote control?" said Alan, fumbling around desperately in the bushes. "I need it to detonate the **BOUNCY EXPLODEY BOMB!**"

"Quick!" said Wilf. "We need to find it before they do!"

Wilf and Abi looked around wildly for the remote control too. Dot didn't join in. She was too busy chewing on the remote control. Wait a minute! The remote control! Dot had it!

Alan launched himself at Dot—and Wilf and Abi launched themselves at Alan.

They fought and tussled and struggled and brawled. They walloped and pounded and smacked and clouted, and finally Wilf grabbed the remote control just before Alan knocked it from his hands. It bounced down the riverbank and landed with a **PLOP** in the water.

Wilf was about to wade into the river when he noticed . . . lots and lots of pairs of eyes watching him from the water. The river was FULL of crocodiles. And Wilf was very scared of crocodiles. He stretched a trembling arm for his backpack so he could look at his **"HOW TO STOP WORRYING"** leaflet, but as he did so Alan kicked it out of his hands. The backpack flew high into the air and landed in the wide-open mouth of a crocodile, who gulped it down in one gulp.

Meanwhile, Alan started rolling the

BOUNCY EXPLODEY BOMB toward the top of Victoria Falls.

"Kevin! Fetch the remote!" ordered Alan.

Kevin waded cautiously into the water.

Wilf was horrified. What was he going to do now? His leaflet was gone. The POOBUM was gone. He didn't have anything to help him. He didn't have a plan. And, most of all, he didn't have time to worry. And there was nothing he would have liked more than

to have a big old worry. But he couldn't.
The future of the whole world depended
on him!

Just then a vast crocodile hauled itself
toward Wilf from behind a rock. Wilf was
about to scream when he realized it was
Barry! Wilf wasn't scared of Barry! Barry
was his friend.

"Barry!" said Wilf. "Listen, I know you're
scared of swimming underwater and I'm
scared of swimming underwater too, but we
have to get that remote control back! Will you
help me?"

Barry stared back at Wilf.

"You can't understand me, can you?" said
Wilf sadly.

Barry reached a long scaly claw toward
Wilf's hand.

"You can do it together!" said Abi.

And they did. Wilf and Barry walked hand in claw toward the river and then paddled into the water.

"Ready?" said Wilf. "After three. One, two, three!"

And Wilf and Barry swam together to the bottom of the river.

Only meters away, Alan had rolled

the **BOUNCY EXPLODEY BOMB** into the water near the top of the waterfall.

"Hurry up, Kevin!" shouted Alan. "Once this goes over the edge, I need to detonate it and it will bounce and explode and bounce and explode, destroying everyone and everything in its path!"

Kevin plunged obediently into the water.

But there was a problem. The **BOUNCY EXPLODEY BOMB** seemed to be stuck.

"Why isn't it rolling?" said Alan, exasperated. He kicked it a few times. Something seemed to be in its way. In fact, it was not something, but several somethings. Dozens of somethings. Michelle the hippo and all her hippo friends had lined up across the river, forming a huge hippo dam.

"Damn!" said Alan.[*]

At that moment, Wilf and Barry surged and spluttered up to the surface of the river, remote control in hand.

"Aaaargh!" screamed Alan. "A crocodile!"

Wilf and Barry started swimming back to the riverbank.

"You did it! You did it!" cried Abi.

"This is not fair! You're all ganging up against me!" said Alan, shaking his fist.

Just then, Kevin burst up through the water, grabbed the remote from Wilf's hands with his teeth, and doggy paddled furiously toward Alan.

"Good boy!" said Alan taking the remote control. "Now you shall all die! For I will detonate my **BOUNCY EXPLODEY BOMB** and everyone and everything will—"

* **Correct.**

Dot clapped her hands in delight and Wilf quickly grabbed the remote control from Alan's hands. He threw it to Susan, then Susan and all her elephant friends stomped on it.

Colin the snake and Abi led all the sick snakes to safety across the hippos' backs. Michelle and the other hippos pushed the remains

of the **BOUNCY EXPLODEY BOMB** to the riverbank, where all the tiny birds who liked to balance on the hippos' heads picked it apart—until all that was left was a pile of springs and wires and nuts and bolts.

"My bomb! My beautiful bomb!" wailed Alan from within his ball of dung.

Susan the elephant took pity on Alan and squirted all the dung off him with her trunk.

Alan turned to Kevin sadly. "You are my only friend, Kevin," he said. "You are the most loyal right-hand man in the world."

Kevin wagged his tail very hard. Then Alan and Kevin went back to the hotel and ate those biscuits that were at the bottom of the green bag.

Wilf and Dot and Abi and Stuart all went back to the jungle and celebrated together, singing songs and dancing.

"Do you know something, Abi?" said Wilf. "I've changed my mind. I do like animals."

"I've changed my mind too," said Abi. "I like people. Well, one person in particular."

Abi gave Wilf a big hug, and Wilf went very pink indeed.

THE END

Not this again . . .

You **KNOW** it's the **END** of the book!

Go away!

OK, OK, if you **REALLY** want another adventure with **WILF**, get hold of these brilliant books...

Wilf's first worrisome adventure with Alan

Alan has decided to be a pirate! What could possibly go wrong?

and the

ALIEN INVASION

Alan wants to destroy Mars?

NOOOOOOOOOO!

Coming soon

wilfthemightyworrier.com